Curious George®

GOES CAMPING

Adapted from the Curious George film series
Edited by Margret Rey and Alan J. Shalleck

1 9 9 0
Houghton Mifflin Company, Boston

Library of Congress Cataloging-in-Publication Data

Curious George goes camping/edited by Margret Rey and
   Alan J. Shalleck.
      p. cm.
   "Adapted from the Curious George film series."
   Summary: Curious George gets into mischief while camping but is able
to redeem himself in an emergency.
   ISBN 0-395-55726-7
   [1. Monkeys—Fiction. 2. Camping—Fiction.] I. Rey, Margret.
II. Shalleck, Alan J. III. Curious George goes camping (Motion picture)
PZ7.C921365   1990   90-33224
[E]—dc20   CIP
                    AC

Printed in the United States of America

RNF ISBN 0-395-55726-7
PAP ISBN 0-395-55715-1

WOZ 10 9 8 7 6 5 4 3 2 1

George and his friend, the man with the
yellow hat, were going on a camping trip.

A ranger greeted them at the entrance of the park. "Have a great time," he told them.

They drove to a lake.
"Here's a good spot to set up camp, George,"
said the man with the yellow hat.

"Let's get unpacked," he said to George.

"I'll go get some water to cook with.
You can look around, George,
but don't get into trouble."

George went exploring. At one campsite,
George saw a man cooking some fish for his
family. Mmmm! It smelled good.

At another campsite a girl was pouring
water over a campfire.

"I want to make sure it's completely out,"
she told George.
"One spark could start a whole forest fire."

George walked on until he saw a small tent.

Inside was a thin pole standing
right in the middle.

Suddenly George heard footsteps.
Someone was coming!

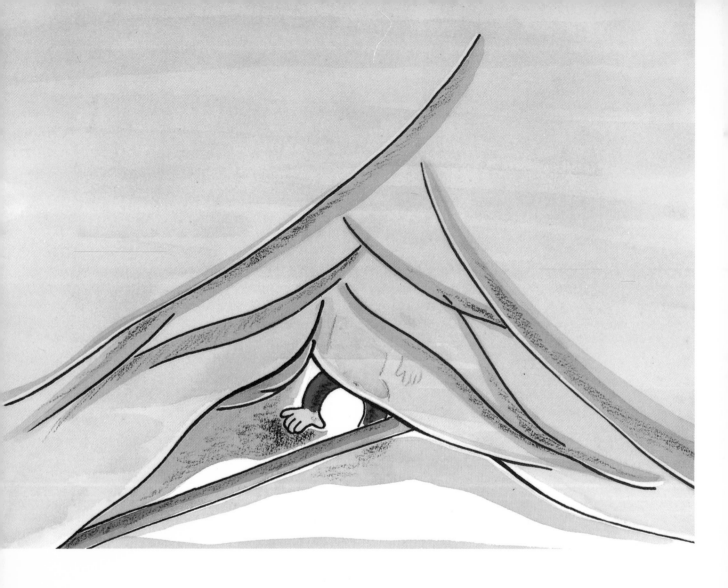

He jumped into the tent and
knocked over the pole.

"Who's in there?" a man shouted.
"Come out right now!" He was angry.

George crawled out and ran away.
The man ran after him.

George climbed to the top of a tall tree.
Now he was safe.

From the tree he could see
the man in the yellow hat returning to the
campsite with a bucket of water.

Then George saw something scary –
smoke coming from an empty campsite.
Fire!!

George had to stop the fire,
and he knew just what to do.

He climbed down and ran to get the bucket
of water from his own campsite.

George grabbed the bucket
and ran past the other campers.
"Where's that monkey going?" a camper shouted.

"Daddy, I see smoke," yelled a little girl.

The man with the yellow hat
came rushing out of his tent.
"Fire!" he yelled. "Quick, let's go."

Everyone ran after George.

George dumped his bucket on the fire.

Everybody helped pour water
on the fire until it was out.

The ranger came to see what had happened.
So did the man whose tent had fallen down.

"Good job, George," he said.
"Sorry I was angry at you."

"You're a real fine scout," said the ranger.
"Hooray for George!" everyone shouted.

George and the man with the yellow hat went
back to their campsite to have dinner.

"George," said the man with the yellow hat,
"you did all right today."